I0843502

SPOOKABOO

Karen

Copyright © 2024 Karen

All rights reserved.

No part of this book may be reproduced, stored in a retrieval system, or transmitted, in any form or by any means, electronic, mechanical, photocopying, recording, or otherwise, without prior written permission from the publisher, except for brief quotations embodied in critical reviews and certain other noncommercial uses permitted by copyright law.

ISBN: 978-1-965666-34-0

Printed in the United States of America

Contents

Chapter 1

After 6 weeks in rehab, Andy was done, it's not that Andy didn't appreciate the staff, all the doctors, physical therapist, nurses and the aides, when he got here, he couldn't walk, could barely speak. Even though he still used a wheelchair, the rehab got him walking again, slowly but still walking and his speech has come a long way. Now, it's time to go home, he missed his Maine Coon Betsy and his German Shepherd Abby, who were being cared for by Jesse's family. The person he missed most was Vee, even though she came to the rehab everyday, he just wanted to go home with her and tell her, how much he loved her. Vee meant the world to him, Andy actually felt guilty that he put her through the last couple of months. Knowing that he was not 100 %, Vee took a leave of absence. When her boss told Vee, that she couldn't hold her job open because it was a small shop, Vee gave her notice. Andy wasn't happy with that but Vee said it would be okay.

" I get to spend my days, with the handsomest guy in Poland."
Andy couldn't have loved her more, she was his true love.

The doctor at the rehab, came into the room, he was a younger guy, very soft spoken, the more Andy got to know him, the more Andy grew leery of him. Call it his reporter's intuition or gut feeling, I don't trust him, Andy thought to himself.

" How are we feeling today, Mr Levesque?"

" I'm doing okay."

" So you feel that, you are well enough to continue your rehabilitation at home and we will be sending a nurse to check on you a couple days a week. It's really important to keep up with all the methods that you learned here, especially the diabetes treatment."

Andy nodded.

" You have someone, at home that will be caring for you? We do not like to send stroke victims home, by themselves. You have been through a lot."

" Yes."

" They will be with you 24 hours a day? "

Andy nodded again.

" Okay, then the nurse will be coming in to go over your medication and your discharge papers. Any questions for me?"

" Will I make a full recovery?"

"Yeah, well there's no reason why you wouldn't be going back to doing, what you were before everything happened. However, your body has been through hell and back, sorry for the bluntness of that statement. It's not like we can guarantee anything. Just keep doing what was told to you, in all your appointments, if you continue to do that, you should be fine. Anything else? "

Andy shook his head, No.

Vee knocked on the door.

The doctor waved her in, he then continued, asking Vee if she had any questions.

Vee couldn't understand, what happened to Andy, he was a relatively healthy guy, so if he was following his diabetes medication and everything, what happened.

" To explain in layman's terms, his body was storing too much glucose in his arteries, they got damaged, possibly loosing a blood clot that traveled to his brain. Of course, the other thing was the heart attack and other small strokes. It's not a matter of how healthy and how well he took care of himself, Andy's diabetes, it's his body's doing.

Has he had any, stress in his life right now? Stress elevates blood sugar."

"Maybe, I could think of a few things bothering him."

"Try to eliminate those situations, he will benefit from that. Any other questions? You can call me or his regular doctor, anytime. He came a long way, he was a very very lucky man."

They thanked the doctor again, then Andy and Vee collected Andy' s belongings and headed for the door. Andy was still self conscious about the wheelchair, but he was getting better at it.

"Do you mind if I say Goodbye, to a few people? "

"Where to?"

"The dining room! "

Andy had Vee push him over to an elderly lady, she looked frail, when she looked up, the kindness in her eyes shined right through.

"Hi Valerie" Andy's voice was warm, with a loving tone.

Valerie took to Andy when he first started coming to the dining room. Andy and Valerie were almost inseparable, when Vee left for the night, Andy asked a tech, if he can hang out in Valerie's room. The two watched tv together, chatted, even snoozed until the tech came to get Andy.

"Andy, Vee hello. The big day!"

Andy beamed, Valerie become almost like a mother to him.

"Yup, I'm going home to drive Vee nuts!"

Vee kissed the top of Andy's head.

"I'm happy for you, Andy. I'll miss our late night tv sessions."

"I'm going to come back and visit Valerie, as soon as the doctor, says it's okay to go out and about. Right now, I'm pretty restricted to being home, getting better. I will text you though, if that's okay."

Valerie stood and walked over to Andy.

" Bless your heart, of course, it's okay. It's more than okay, you would be making an old lady smile again."

The two new friends hugged and kissed.

Valerie turned to Vee, gave her a quick hug.

"You take care of him, you hear.

I can't wait until he's well enough, so I can see you both."

"I will, I promise." Vee said.

Valerie went back to her group and Andy and Vee left the dining area.

"Can we go to the front desk, Vee"

" Of course, honey."

At the front desk, was one of the most handsomest men, Vee ever saw. Tall, light skinned black man, broad shoulders and eyes that could read your soul. Andy chuckled.

" You can stop drooling now, babe."

Vee blushed " I was not"

"Yeah right."

The man turn and saw them.

" Andy, Vee!"

"Hey Cody! Just coming to say bye."

Cody came around and shook

hands with Andy. Cody was Andy's physical therapist, the two men bonded, talking about current events and sports once Andy started speaking again.

"You be sure to follow up on those exercises, I taught you, brother. Don't make Vee call me."

Cody winked at Vee, who blushed. Andy laughed.

"Are you kidding, she'd love that."

Vee gave Andy a light punch, which made both guys laugh.

"Take care, you two."

Andy went to see a couple more people, then it was time to go.

"Ready?" Vee asked.

Andy blew out a deep breath.

"Ready!"

Chapter 2

Benny tried really hard to quiet his mind, he did not want to rush back to work, working a job, that he wasn't passionate about. In his head, Benny knew, as much as he loved police work, it wasn't the same as being out in the field. The firefighter thing, I just can't see myself doing that, it's a really noble job, I have tons of respect for it, but I think I'm more of a lone wolf. Living in a house with 20 other people, who are not my family, imagine the trouble, I could get in. I have my law degree, but Oliver was right, on that, me sitting behind a desk for 10-12 hours, nope.

"Benny?"

Benny nearly jumped out of his skin, a very unusual reaction for him.

"Dad, you scared the crap, out of me "

Paul laughed, he couldn't help it, his youngest son, was anything but timid. In school, he used to be known as the bully killer. Benny wasn't afraid of anything, it was a little funny for him to be jumping out of his chair, when Paul called him.

" What is the matter, son?"

"Nothing dad, I was just deep in thought."

" How's everything going, still looking into the police department?"

Benny looked at his father, and sighed.

" I don't think law enforcement is for me anymore, no firefighting

either."

"Well, why does it have to be a service thing. Look at Andy, he went to work in an antique toy store, it makes him happy. What makes you happy Benny? "

" I don't know, funny cause Oliver mentioned opening a gym, I even thought about that, I just.." his voice trailed off.

" You know Benny, Max could use some help in the stables, just to keep yourself busy, you might consider it."

" Mucking stalls?"

" It's honest work, clear your mind."

" I'll think about it, Dad, it's not a terrible idea, I do like the horses."

"Great, just let Max know, what you decide."

" Where you heading, Dad? Anything exciting?"

" Lynne, is getting all these weird cravings now, something about olives and beef Terriyaki."

Benny laughed, he was truly happy for his father, finding love again and creating new life.

" You know those don't come in the same store. Want some company?"

" Really? Of course. "

"You know I'm only going so you will buy me, some Chinese food too."

Paul laughed.

" Of course, a father's wallet never closes."

The ride was longer than Benny expected, dad must really love Lynne or he is trying to get out of the house, Benny thought to himself.

"Yes, I'm trying to get away from my future wife."

Benny laughed.

" Wow! Did I think out loud?"

" No, but it's what I'd have been thinking. The hormone swings are driving me crazy enough to drive 9 miles to pick up Chinese food."

" Aww, young love."

" Yeah, right. Benny, what happened with you and Oliver, I thought it was good."

" It was, until it wasn't. I don't know dad, I think it was his pushing."

" nagging?"

" I guess, I'm a grown man, I've lived in hellholes of Colombia, bullets zinging past my head. My feelings were Ollie wasn't prepared to compromise, even if he said he was."

Paul nodded.

" Ollie, Oliver, I did love him, but I wasn't enough in love with him to marry him. That's what he wanted, hell, I couldn't get him to understand, we weren't even together that long, y'no? Was I wrong?"

Paul shook his head.

" Son, I chased Oliver back to you, maybe that was wrong."

" No, no , it would have eventually happened, I was going to call him, it's just meant to be this way." Benny let out a sigh.

" Maybe."

They rode in silence, got to the Chinese food place. They picked up enough Chinese food to feed a small army, plus 2 beef teriyakis.

Benny fiddled with the radio while Paul drove, Paul looked over, he didn't see his 27 year old son, a grown man, he saw his 13 year old son fiddling with the radio, as they were going home from one of their many fishing trips. Paul remembered one time

" Dad, can I tell you something "

his thirteen year old son said.

"Anything , anytime."

" I think I'm different."

" What do you mean, different Benny?"

" I don't like girls, like Jesse."

" You're still young."

Paul realized he was talking to a 13 year old with raging hormones.

" No, Dad, I think, I think I'm gay.

I get feelings around some boys."

Trying not to stereotype, It was hard to image Benny being gay, he was a rugged sort, when Jesse and Benny had there arguments, it was Benny who came out on top, literally. At 13 he stood eye to eye with Paul.

" It's okay son, you figure out, who you are and your mom and I, we will always be in your corner because we love you.."

13 year old Benny smiled up from the radio.

"Dad" 27 year old Benny snapped his father out of his reverie .

"Mmmm"

"Stop dreaming about the Chinese food . "

Paul laughed.

The ride back was like a site seeing tour for Benny, his father showed him places that were new to him. Such a beautiful place, Maine was.

" Dad."

Paul looked over at Benny.

" There was more to what happened with Oliver."

" Mmmm."

Of course, his father knew, Paul Wiseman was the ultimate cop, you could not get anything past him.

"There was a woman in South America."

Benny's voice trailed off almost like a whisper, a secret.

Paul looked over at his youngest child, he was 18 now, tears streaming down his face, his first break up. Benny tried to beat being gay, he had gone out with several girls in high school.

Girls came and went, nothing more than high school flings. Finally, it was unavoidable, Benny met a gay man, a bit older than himself, the man used Benny for sexual pleasure with no concern that the boy was falling hard for him. This affair had gone on for a few months, until the man was bored with Benny and started dating another young man. Benny couldn't bare to be around anymore, the hurt too painful,he needed to get away from his town, where this man lived. He joined the service and was out of there in a week. Paul remembered, his young son fresh out of graduation heading into the service, not to serve his country but to run away from a monster.

" Her name was Ana, I think I was in love with her, I know I was in love with her, I think I still am, that's why when Oliver said he wanted to get married, I knew I had to end it. I mean, we hadn't even dated six months, what was he thinking?"

"Ana?" Paul tried to keep his eyes on the road and his voice steady.

"So many times, I wanted to call her just to hear her voice. You must think I'm crazy."

Paul shook his head, no.

" Why would I think that?"

" I dated guys and fell in love with a woman. I feel like a fraud."

Paul pulled over.

" A fraud? Benny when people date, they look for a mate. Someone, that completes them. In your case, being bisexual, you had to test both waters."

Benny nodded.

" Thanks dad."

" Call Ana."

" She lives in Bolivia. I can't move to Bolivia."

"Just talk to her."

Benny and Paul got home, Lynne didn't even greet them, grabbed her Terriyaki and headed for the couch.

"Lynne, honey, do you want anything else, we almost bought out the place."

"Nah, oh hi Benny."

Benny looked at Paul, Paul chuckled, and nodded.

" Hi Lynne, how you feeling?"

" Like a beached whale."

Lynne was only 4 months, but had already gained a lot of weight, doctor said it, could be because she was a little older.

Of course, that doctor, will never again call an expectant mother older again.

" Ok, I'm going to go take a quick shower and wait for the others, to eat."

Paul made a dialing gesture.

" Call her."

Lynne perked up. " Call who?"

Benny ducked into the other room. Not today, he thought to himself, not today.

Chapter 3

"Tiny, Moose yummies!" Maddie yelled

Moose, the tiny teacup poodle came running to Maddie. Maddie waited, then yelled again "Tiny!" Tiny, Maddie's 125 plus pound Bernese Mountain dog was no where to be seen.

" Moose where's Tiny? Show me."

Moose headed for the back of the house, there Maddie found Tiny laying on his side.

" TINY!"

But the dog didn't respond, Maddie's heart stopped Tiny wasn't old, he was in good health his last check up. Please move she thought to herself.

Dorie, Maddie's future sister-in-law came out on the back porch.

" Maddie, what's wrong ? "

"Tiny is not moving" Maddie said as she slowly went to Tiny, fearing the worse, hoping for the best, he could be sound asleep.

As she got closer, Tiny turned his head toward her and wagged his tail slowly, but wouldn't stand up.

"Tiny come here."

The monster dog tried to get up, Moose started yapping at both Maddie and Tiny, like he was telling Tiny to stay down. Kneeling on the ground next to Tiny, Maddie saw the blood.

" Dorie, get your dad and Benny, It looks like Tiny's been shot."

Dorie rushed in the house, screaming for her dad. Paul came rushing out with Benny on his heels.

" Maddie, what's going on?" Then he saw Tiny.

Lynne came out and told the group, she already called the vet and he was expecting them.

" I called Max too, he's bringing the pickup."

Tiny heard Lynne, his best human friend since she moved in. His tail started going like crazy and he tried to get up, she ran over to him. Moose started yapping at Lynne and Tiny now, like he was in charge.

Lynne tried to hold Tiny down.

" Good boy Tiny, stay down Max is coming."

Tiny's head swiveling, like where, where is Max.

Seconds later, Max zoomed up the road. The three men, loaded the big dog into the back of the pickup truck, covered with blankets.

" Maddie let's go." Max yelled.

As quick as he got there, Max shot out of site.

The rest were left, standing there wondering just what happened. Lynne broke the silence.

" So help my Lord, when I find out who shot that dog, they better hope I'm not carrying my gun." With that she stormed into the house, Moose trailing after her.

Leaving the three Wisemans looking at each other over what they just heard her say. So unLynne like.

Benny said what the rest were thinking.

" I wouldn't want to be that person."

Dorie and Paul nodded.

Max and Maddie got to the vet's office, Jesse, Maddie's fiancée was already there. Jesse was Poland's Sheriff, getting out of his squad car, he ran over to the back of the pickup.

" It's going to be okay Tiny, Dr Trey is going to patch up that boo-boo."

Tiny tried standing again, Jesse swooped him up, like he was light as a feather.

" Come on, boy, yes yes I love you too. " As Tiny tried to give Jesse kisses.

They got Tiny inside, the technician Mabel got the rolling table.

" Tiny? What happened?"

Mabel looked at Tiny's humans.

Maddie had to catch her breath, so she wouldn't break down.

" I found him, in the backyard, when I got to him, the ground was covered with blood, it looks like he was shot."

The bleeding had slowed down, so now Mabel could look at the wound, Tiny whimpered.

Mabel baby talked Tiny.

" It's okay boy, I'm just taking a look."

Mabel looked at Maddie.

"BB pellet, but looks like it hit an artery. Trey will tie it off, I believe, the worse is over, most likely need some antibiotics and painkillers.

Someone needs to find that shooter. Most likely a kid, whose parents let them take the gun out unsupervised."

Maddie fell into Jesse.

" It's okay Mads, Trey's going to take care of Tiny. Max have you seen any kids out that way?"

" Not unfamiliar ones, some come to the stables, I let them pet the horses, Nobody should be out there without permission, your land spreads far and wide.

I hate to say it, thieves could have been trying to put Tiny out of commission, he's a big watch dog. "

Jesse thought about that.

Trey came out, gave Maddie a hug and shook the guys hands.

"Okay, so Tiny got a BB pellet lodged, in his upper right hind leg, which is why you saw so much blood. He probably tried to keep standing with more and more blood coming out, he just gave up. I got the pellet out, stitched him up, I can keep him for observation because of the blood loss or you can take him home but someone will need to keep watch on him for 24 to 48 hours depending how he does on the antibiotics."

Jesse knew the answer before Maddie could speak.

" We'll take him home, there is a lot of people in our house, we can do shifts."

Maddie nodded. Trey went on.

"We can put a classic cone or you can grab one of those soft ones in the gift shoppe, free of charge."

Maddie went to pay, Jesse went for soft cone, Max loaded Tiny with the help of Mabel.

"Take care of my Tiny, Max."

" You know we will Mabel, I just hope we find the shooter, that's dangerous."

" Most times, it's unsupervised kids. Image if that was someone's child? Not that Tiny is not Maddie's fur baby, like you said it's dangerous."

On the way home, Maddie rode in truck bed with Tiny. Jesse spoke through the back window.

" I'm not even sure how to go about finding this person. A lot of kids have BB guns, they shoot cans and bottles, most parents supervise them. If it were so close to the house, I'd say it was a wild shot."

Maddie looked at Jesse.

" Why would anyone want to shoot Tiny? All the neighbors' kids love him."

Max eyes on the road.

" Sorry but I don't think this was kids, maybe older late aged teenagers, lots of groups around here, could be a dare."

" Dare someone to shoot my dog."

Max sighed

" I don't know Maddie, farmers see it all the time. Goats, pigs cows, chickens . These groups make up the stupidest cruelest initiations."

" Cult?" Jesse asked.

" No, I don't think they are cults,

bored teenagers, getting with the wrong people. I can't even say that's it, just a thought."

Tiny whimpered. Maddie hugged him close.

" I know baby, we are going to get you home and give you the painkiller."

The rest of the ride was in silence.

When Max pulled up to the house, Lynne came running out, Moose behind her.

She pulled the truck bed door open and reached for Tiny.

" How's my boy?" Moose barked in back of her.

Tiny wagged his tail. Maddie took a deep breath.

" It looks like he's going to be okay, Trey removed a BB pellet."

Maddie then asked Lynne, what she thought about Max' idea.

" You know that's possible, it's a new school year, kids meet new friends, friends who look for trouble. It's not a bad theory."

They got Tiny in the house, put him in his bed, Moose curled into his midsection, they went to sleep.

Dorie said she kept supper warm.

" Come on everyone, you guys must be starving."

They went into the dining room, Dorie made beef stew, it made the house smell heavenly.

"Dig in."

Paul watched Max, his young friend was troubled. Max, who was usually chatty with the ladies, sat quietly eating, at times shaking his head.

"What's up? Max, you're very quiet." The elder Wiseman asked

" I just feel, I just feel responsible for Tiny."

Maddie's head snapped up.

"Max, you are almost 2 miles from house, please don't feel that way."

" I heard other ranchers talking,

trouble with these, punks, I watched the stable. I never thought about the dogs or cats."

" Not another thought, I would never blame you for something like that. I just wanted to the person responsible, really responsible. Do you really think it's bored teenagers?"

Max sighed.

" I want to say yes, but even the

dumbest teenagers around here, know and respect Sheriff Wiseman. Maybe someone with a grudge."

" Now, there's a thought " Paul said.

They all agreed.

Dorie looked at her family, worried no one would get any sleep tonight.

" Let's all just settle down, for the night, Tiny's doing okay, his nurse Moose is comforting him."

Moose looked up, comically, it looked like he nodded in agreement.

Chapter 4

The phone trilled in Benny's ear, his heart raced and suddenly all the air went out of the room.

" Benny?"

She still had him in her contacts,

His heart was in his throat, he suddenly felt like no words would come out, if he tried to speak .

" Benny are you there?"

Benny cleared his throat, and found his voice.

" Hi Ana."

" Oh Benny, I'm so happy to hear from you. I've missed you. How are you?"

" I'm good, how are things in Bolivia?"

There was a long pause.

" Benny, I'm not in South America, I'm in the States. I'm living in Mass., Boston actually.

Benny's heart did a flip.

" What?"

" Benny, we need to talk, I tried to find you, but seem to always a dead end."

" Why didn't you call me?"

" I wanted to tell you in person. Can we get together, maybe one day this week?"

"Tomorrow?"b

" That's my Benny, the go getter."

Bennys heart pounded against his chest. My Benny.

"What's going on,Ana. Are you okay?"

" I'm fine Benny, I just need to tell you something. I'm glad you called."

"God, Ana now I want to see you today.. now"

" Calm down, all is good. There is a seafood place in Rochester, on Portland St., I'll text you the name, meet me there at noon."

" Okay, Ana.."

" I miss you too Benny, I'll text you later okay?"

" Okay."

How the heck am I going to wait til tomorrow, I'll be climbing the walls and up all night.

Benny went into the kitchen to grab a cup of coffee and he wanted to check on Tiny.

Getting his coffee and going into the family room, Maddie was sitting with Tiny and Moose. Dorie came from the outside through the back door.

Benny sat down next to Maddie,

he really liked Maddie, he thought she was good for Jesse, real down to earth, kind and caring.

Dorie sat on the couch, facing them.

" How's he doing?" Benny asked Maddie, she laughed.

" I think he likes the extra attention, I'm guessing he's going to be okay. Trey said he was going to make a full recovery."

Dorie studied her brother, Benny caught her watching him.

"What?"

" You are hiding something."

" You're crazy." Benny said, not very convincingly.

" Out with it Bennerd."

Bennerd was the name, Dorie used to get to Benny, and Jessass to get to Jesse.

" I have no idea, what you are talking about Crazy woman."

" Now, Bennerd, you know you cannot keep secrets from me, look at me."

Benny looked away. Dorie went and stood in front of him.

" Bennerd"

Again, Benny ignored her, Dorie was getting frustrated. Maddie could see, and trying to help.

" Benny, I noticed too, that it seemed like you had something to share."

" It's no big deal, MADDIE, I'm meeting an old friend tomorrow."

Dorie laughed.

" That's it, I knew it, you had a glow, what's his name?"

Benny ignored her, Maddie laugh, she loved Jesse's crazy family, she tapped him on his shoulder.

" Who is it?"

"Her name is Ana."

Maddie and Dorie looked at each other.

Dorie had enough.

"Ana? What are you meeting her for? Where, what's the big secret?"

" There's no secret, me and Ana dated for awhile, we broke up when I came home after my assignment. I called her yesterday. She told me, she had something to tell me, in person."

Men are so dense, Dorie thought, but didn't tell Benny what she thought. Looking at Maddie, who nodded.

" Okay."

"Okay? You are not going to hound me for details?"

" Oh no, I'm good, where you meeting HER?"

" Couldn't put that past you, huh Sis?

Jesse came in, Lynne waddling behind him. He looked at his family.

" What's going on?"

Dorie blurted out.

" Benny's meeting a woman he dated while he was on assignment. She needs to tell him something. "

" How much you owe her, Ben?"

Jesse laughed at his own joke.

The three women just looked at him, like he had three heads.

" So what you're leaving?"

" No, Jesse, she's been living in Boston, I called her yesterday and she told me that she had something to tell me that's it."

Lynne said. " Doesn't seem she tried so hard to tell you, if she still had your number and living in the next state."

That kind of bothered Benny, too.

" So where is this meeting ?"

"Seabrook , some restaurant."

Dorie jumpes up.

" I'm coming with the kids."

"I would too, but I don't want to leave Tiny and Moose." Maddie said.

Lynne responded. " I'll watch the boys, Maddie you can go for the ride. It will do you all good."

Maddie said thank you.

The front door swung open. Paul took his jacket off.

" A little bit of a northeaster out there."

He looked at his family, they all looked like they were guilty of something, he chuckled.

" Now what?"

So they all started talking at the same time, telling him about Benny's big adventure. From the look on his face, the ladies knew Paul, had the same idea as they had .

"That's great, Benny, of course, unless you owe money."

The ladies groaned.

" See, my father gets it." Jesse laughed. Everyone started laughing.

The next day, the loaded up the car, Lynne came over to Benny.

" Be careful, I still don't get, she had something to tell you and never called you."

She gave her future stepson, a kiss on the cheek.

Paul grabbed the seat of her pants, "Alright officer, remember, he was a federal agent. "

Everyone laughed.

Driving down to Seabrook, Benny got a little anxious, thinking what it could possibly be that Ana needed to tell him.

Maybe she got married, most likely just wanted to catch up.

Ana was a free spirit, you never know what she was up to one day to the next.

The restaurant, was seafood, like a diner with outdoor seating.

Benny parked, they got out, Dorie and Maddie took the kids straight in the restaurant, so the could settle and order, before Benny even strolled in.

Benny went inside and looked around, he spotted Ana, he waved, she got up and went to over to him. Well, it wasn't hard for Benny to tell, what it was she wanted to talk about.

Chapter 5

Andy was restless, he hated the being in the wheelchair, he couldn't even go to shop, the stupid contraption was too wide.

The doctor suggested he'd get out, even it was to reconnect with old friends. Ha! Old friends last time, I saw an old friend.

Vee was watching Andy, she knew he was really depressed.

Andy was lucky to be alive but she felt that even this wasn't enough. I want to motivate him,

Vee thought to herself, Andy was usually the last person that need motivation. Andy was known to wake up in the morning and go climb mountains, but after the diabetes scare, the only climbing he did was, into bed. Banging into another wall, Andy swore, everyone looked to his direction.

" Sorry" he muttered to no one in particular.

" Baby, it's okay, just slow down, you have plenty of time."

" Slow down? I already feel like I in reverse." Andy shook his head. " I can't do this, Vee. This is not me, I need my legs, I need to stand, walk, run, jog, climb, I need those things, Vee. "

A young voice behind them, blurted out.

" Oh, boo hoo, listen to the old man crying. He can't walk. Is it permanent, maybe take a look around you at the people, who have no hope at ever walking again. Of course, you might be here for 6 months you don't need to make friends here."

Vee and Andy looked at the young man, who spoke so calmly but with anger of a dozen men. Tyler was as calm a kid could be, when he leveled his gaze at Andy.

"Stop complaining, you look like you ain't too bad off."

Andy took offense.

" Look kid.. "

" I'm not a kid, I'm 21. "

" Still the disrespect.."

" I hate complainers, fine I jumped on you, I apologize, look you look well fed, well dressed, you are probably in here for therapy, it temporary. Some are in here, because they will never walk again. They learn to adapt. You, you just bellyache these patients do not need to hear, your sob story. Okay. No disrespect."

Vee stretched out her hand.

" I'm Vee, this is Andy. He's usually not this grumpy."

Andy threw up his hands.

" I'm sorry, man. I hate this chair."

"Andy, roll over here.

Andy rolled to where Tyler was sitting, the young man was in shorts revealing his artificial limbs. It was Andy's turn to look into Tyler's eyes ."

" You're Tyler Juneau. All Pro Wrestler. Man, what happened?"

" I wanted to join to WWE, cause I loved the excitement, I wasn't a 9-5 er you know. Weird thing, my injury wasn't wrestling related. The wrestling school, I joined, a bunch guys trying to impress some chicks with pick up football game. I was tackled from the back, spine injury, was bad. They amputated. Here, I am."

" I'm sorry."

" No, it's God's will, everything

happens for a reason."

" Look man, I know we started out bad, but I'd really like to

keep in touch."

Tyler looked at Andy.

" A friend out of pity?"

"Tyler, are you kidding, right now, you're a better athlete than

me.. still."

Tyler smiled, they shook hands and exchanged information. The

nurse came for Tyler, he turned back to Andy.

" Hey Crash, watch the walls."

Andy and Vee laughed.

Another nurse came for Andy.

" Mr Levesque."

" That's me."

Chapter 6

Benny couldn't get over he was going to be a father. He knew he could have always adopt, but here he was, it was a weird and wonderful feeling. Ana let him feel the baby kicked, it almost sent him to the moon.

"What do you have in there a future soccer star? " Ana laughed, a tear ran down her cheek.

Benny looked at her, he was puzzled.

" Whats wrong?"

" Nothing, I'm happy"

"Marry me?"

" Benny, you don't have to do that."

" I know that, doesn't mean I don't want to."

She looked deep into the eyes of her best friend, her lover. " Yes.

Yes, I will."

"You will, oh baby, thank God, I thought .."

" You thought what?"

" I thought you'd say no."

Ava laughed

"Benny Wiseman, I love you."

"I love you too, I'm going to ask dad if you can set up in one of the cottages til we …"

Benny stopped in mid-sentence, he saw the look on Ana's face.

"Ana?"

"Benny, I wanted to have the baby in Bolivia."

Benny looked slapped in the face.

" Ana, come on."

"It's my home, Benny, I'm only in the states , for my job,"

" What about us? You can get a job here."

"Here? Benny, half the time there's not even proper WiFi, look you know how important my career is. Come back to Bolivia."

" I dunno know, Ana, I left that all behind, it was part of my job, that I'd like to forget."

The minute the words were out, Benny knew that he couldn't take them back. He looked at Ana.

" I see."

" That's not what I meant."

" Was I part, of your Job, would we, be here today, if it wasn't for your job?"

" Ana."

"Benny, I'm going to go, I need some time to think, so don't you.

I leave for Bolivia in a week."

"Ana, don't do this."

" You knew who, I was, you knew where my home was. You should have left me alone. Maybe, your hunger, your selfishness, will come back to bite you, in the ass."

"Selfishness?" That stung.

" Bye Benny."

Ana turned and walked away.

Benny felt like he grew roots, out of his feet. He loved Ana, but not Bolivia.

Doris ran up to Benny

" Go after her, Ben."

" Dorie."

" Benny, Benny what are you doing? Why would you chase her down only to throw it away."

" Dorie."

"No, Why can't you for once in your life, just jump."

"The baby's not mine."

Maddie came over and both women looked at Benny.

" I didn't come straight here, I did go to Minnesota , I stayed there a couple of months, I told Auntie Mary, that it needed to be, our little secret. I wasn't in Bolivia, the timings not right. Then she said she came looking for me, in Minnesota. She lied, I was in Minnesota, nobody came to see me.

" Why didn't you come here, why'd you stay in Minnesota?"

" Dorie, I was shot, my assignment wasn't over, I was sent home. One more inch and I wouldn't have been here. When Auntie Mary told me, where you were and that she was watching the house. I swore her to secrecy and holed up there to heal. I came here, you guys had that festival, I met Oliver, but the pull of the chase, I went back to work. The assignment was over, but they wanted to put me right back in Bolivia. I couldn't unsee that bullet hitting me in the chest.

Dorie gasped. She realized what he meant now . One more inch and I wouldn't have been here. One more inch.

"I told my captain, he told me, I was done. I didn't come back for Oliver. All those jobs, I thought I'd take, I knew I couldn't do them.

Now, Ana showed up pregnant, I

knew the baby wasn't mine, why the hell, did I ask her to marry me. I don't know what I'm running from. Dor, I'm scared."

Dorie took her brother in her arms, they both fell to their knees, she cradled his head against her chest. Her little baby brother, she held him tight, she was always his protector against booboos and bullies. When their mother died, Dorie took charge of her brothers, now one of them was hurting and she tried to comfort him.

Maddie kneeled down to be with them, stroking Benny's hair, she told him, it was going to get better. Benny sobbed louder. He hadn't cried, after he was shot, his captain told Benny that the therapist was clearing him against his better judgment. The doctor simply said, " he's not ready."

Benny's captain needed him, he asked the doctor, if Benny could perform his duty.

" Special agent Wiseman can be cleared physically to perform his duty. Asking me, if he is mentally fit to do his duty, I'm not going to put that in my report . He was shot, you know as well as I do that, that young man was as good as dead, had that shot been one inch over. What do you think that does to a person? Special Agent Wiseman is in denial, captain, he yet to address the actually incident and when questioned about it, he changes the subject. I'm submitting my report, my hope is no one over looks the fact, that I didn't clear him mentally fit."

Benny was cleared and sent to Bolivia,his first day back a bullet flashed past his head. He called his captain that night, who pulled Benny and sent him home. To Auntie Mary, his childhood home, his bedroom, where every night tried to forget the moment the bullet hit his vest, the kickback. Trying to forget , looking down to see how close the bullet was to center of his chest.

Trying to forget how he went down 210 lbs 6 '2" and a little gold bullet took him down.

He sobbed in Dorie's arms, so much like his mother, how he loved her for being his and Jesse's rock. Benny reached out for

Maddie, pulled her into their circle. The three of them, on the ground , crying.

Sirens blared, Benny knew they were heading here, someone thought they needed the police.

He looked up, and saw his brother's squad car heading at them. Thank God, Benny thought himself.

Maddie went to talk to Jesse, before he got to Benny.

Jesse tried to walk passed Maddie, she grabbed his arm, almost falling.

"Mads. Let me go, what's wrong with him now? It seem like.."

" Jesse, he was shot (Jesse looked at his brother) in Bolivia.

He was shot dead in the chest, his vest saved him.. one inch over .."

" He never told me that."

" He never told anyone that.

Benny holed away, in Minnesota, before he came to Maine.

This woman Ana, just tried to tell Benny, her baby (Maddie motioned a huge belly) was his."

Jesse looked at Maddie, she shook her head, no"

Jesse let out a huge sigh, baby brother could be the world's biggest drama queen pain in the ass. This had to hurt, he knew Benny wanted to be a father, badly.

Jesse regained his composure, start walking slowly toward Benny, who was finally standing.

As they inched closer, Jesse held out his arms.

"Baby brother."

Benny fell into him, Jesse squeezed so hard, he thought about the little rugrat, that drove him crazy. Jesse couldn't let him go, he wanted to hold Benny til the pain is all gone.

"Benny, stop keeping things from me, it's so hard to love you if you are only half here."

" I don't want to bother you."

"Bother me? Me and Dorie, that's our jobs, to be there for you."

Dorie in tears, nodded.

Benny drew in a huge breath

"Jesse."

Jesse leveled his eyes at Benny.

" It wasn't one inch, it was a quarter of an inch. A quarter of inch from death."

Jesse held Benny again..

" It's gonna be okay, Ben, it didn't happen. You survived.

Maddie and Dorie took Benny home. Jesse went back to work, it was hard to leave Benny like that, but with Lynne out on maternity leave, he needed to be there. It was a very long hard day.

Dorie told Benny to go lay down on the couch, she was going to make some coffee and toast for him.

In the kitchen, Maddie was updating Paul and Lynne, Paul was not believing what had just been told to him. His stomach curled into knots, Benny could drive you crazy, but he has a heart of gold, he would give a stranger the shirt off his back.

Paul could not imagine, if .. he shook his head of the image that was now stuck in his head.

" I have to go talk to Benny."

Dorie moved in front of her father, all 5'2" against his 6'2".

" Daddy, it's been a long day for him. Just, if you need to be with him. Just sit with him, there's no need to talk, about it, right now."

Just like her mother, Paul thought. As usual, Dorie was right.

"Okay."

Paul walked into the parlor, Benny was sound asleep.

" He's sleeping."

Dorie said quietly. "Good."

Chapter 7

Maddie went to check on Tiny,

As she approached the back of the house where the two dogs were staying during the day.

Moose got up from his security post, Maddie honestly believed that if someone had tried to her Tiny, Moose with fight with his tiny teacup poodle body until the end.

"At ease, Moosie, it's Mama."

Moose's whole body wagged.

Tiny picked up his head, and cried. Maddie went over to them, patting Tiny's head , and picking up Moose.

" Were you guys good for Lynne? Did she give you a treat?"

Maddie pulled a treat bag out of her pocket.

" Always, come prepared."

The dogs gobbled up their treats.

Maddie heard a noise along the side of the house. Sounded like someone knocked over a rake.

" Lynne, Dorie? "

No one answer but someone started running, a couple of someone's, they didn't run very far, they ran right into the sheriff.

Jesse grabbed them and dropped them on the ground.

" Who the hell are you?"

They were two older male teenagers. They struggled to their feet, swinging at Jesse, one caught Jesse off guard with an upper cut the his jaw. Jess went down. One of the boys, grabbed the rake and turned on Maddie.

Then there was a loud shot gun going off. There stood Lynne, huge belly looking like pregnant Rambo.

" I'd think twice before taking another step little boy. Drop the rake. "

Jesse got to his feet,shook his head. Cuffing both of them, it suddenly dawned on him.

" Billy?"

Billy's dad James Parks went to prison, Jesse arrested him for bank robbery, more than 5 years ago. Well, apple doesn't fall far from tree.

"What's going on, Billy? Why are you on my property. "

Then he noticed the other boy,

Deacon Jr , his father was another loser. Work, get drunk, go home beat his wife. One night Deac beat the wife, an inch from her death and threw her out of his moving car. Jesse enjoyed catching him, enjoyed punching him in the face, so hard he bled, pushing him into a stone wall over and over til Doug took Jesse off of him.

Jesse looked at the two boys, God help them.

Jesse shoved them in his car.

" Did you shoot our dog?"

" Screw you."

" Oh no, boys you're both of age. Animal cruelty is now a big deal. You both get to go visit, your dads. Thanks for the extra paperwork, tonight."

Jesse was livid. Lynne came over, knowing Jesse was an inch from losing it, she took his chin in her fingers, very motherly like.

" I called Doug, he's doing the transport and your paperwork. You go in the house get cleaned up." Jesse started to argue, but one look from Lynne, before he could take one step, Maddie rushed into his arms. Maddie was in tears.

" Mads, Mads okay okay, shhhh."Jesse held her tight. " Mads come on, everything's fine, why are you crying?"

Loud sobs came from Maddie, as she tried to contain herself.

"Jesse, didn't you hear what they said? " Lynne shotgun was what Jesse heard, but he had to admit the upper cut, caught him so off guard, he lost consciousness for a few seconds, then The blast from the gun.

Dorie and Paul had joined them.

Paul looked at his son, he wanted him to take in the severity of his words.

" Jess, Billy parks threatened you, his words were , say your prayers sheriff, I'm sending you to hell. "

Jesse shook his head.

" Yeah, he was caught, of course he was going to say something like that."

Dorie stepped up to Jesse.

" Jess, it's what Deacon said.

That there was more of them, that they were going to keep coming after you til you're dead."

Maddie started sobbing again.

" Alright Alright Mads, it's going to be alright. " he took her hand and they walked back to the house.

Benny was curled in a ball on the couch. Jesse lifted Benny's head sat down and laid Benny's head in his lap like they use to .

When Benny was small, he was terrified of thunder, Jesse and Dorie did everything, when storms would come to calm him.

Finally, it was this that calm Benny, Jesse held his baby brother.

When Maddie had told him, about Benny getting shot, it was the news Jesse had been waiting for, for years. Jesse hated Benny being undercover, in a land of drug lords, he never understood, why Benny needed to do it. Benny always told Jesse, it was like a calling, someone had to. Benny did his job well, commendations coming out his ears. Until, that day, after being shot, Benny tried to go back, and couldn't, knowing he was an easy target now, a liability.

Benny jerked in his sleep, reaching out his hand, Jesse took hold of it. " Baby brother" he whispered. Benny's breathing settled.

Lynne came over lifting Jesse's face, cleaned up the wound.

" You'll live."

" I hope so, my father knocked up my partner."

They all laughed.

Family, this family.

Everyone sat around, til the ladies decided to make some soup for supper.

They left the guys, soon the three men were snoring in harmony.

"Listen to them, the Boston Symphony Orchestra. " Lynne said.

The three ladies laughed.

Laughter is the best medicine, Lynne thought to herself."

Chapter 8

Vee helped Andy in the truck, he did most of the work, she just kind of boosted him up. As she went to stand up, Andy reached out to her, he took her face in his hands and Vee just looked at him. Andy stared into Vee's eyes, sitting up taller to reach her lips, she lowered herself to him. His kiss was gentle and loving, then hungry, it was the most intimacy, they've had since he's been in the hospital. Ver laid her forehead on his and continued to look into his eyes, looking for meaning.

"What was that for, Stud."

" I'm sorry. "

" Sorry? For what?"

" Come on Vee, I haven't exactly been my happy go lucky self."

Vee pretended to be thinking.

" Really? I hadn't noticed."

Andy chuckled.

Oh thank Goodness, Vee thought to herself. I thought I'd never hear that laugh again. Vee kissed him, with an even more hunger. Andy was breathless. Vee laughed and went to close the door.

" Think about that, on the ride home."

Andy was already thinking, his heart started racing. He turned to Vee, when she got in the car.

" You know you're gonna give me a heart attack?"

" Bet it would be worth it."

Andy threw his eyes to heaven.

When they got home, the animal in Andy, got the best of him, he tried to stand to walk to the bedroom. Stumbling, he fell forward onto the couch. Swearing, as he got himself straightened out. Vee came over.

" What happened?"

" I'm sick and tired of being in that chair. I just wanted to walk into the bedroom. "

" It's okay Andy, it takes time."

" I don't want to take time I want to walk now. I'm gonna nap."

" Excuse me? Oh no, you are not.

You got me all worked up, you're going to get those clothes off."

" Vee." He sighed.

" Andy, Either you take your clothes off, or I'm going to rip them off. "

Andy laughed.

" Think I'm kidding boytoy?"

She straddled his lap and pulled her scrunch off, her hair falling around her. The animal was stirring inside of Andy again. In a low growl.

" You want me?"

" You bet I do."

"Vee" Andy shook his finacee'.

"Babe" Vee looked around for the clock, they must of fell asleep after making love. She reached for the clock . 7 pm.

"Seven, Andy, you need to take your pills."

" I know"

" We slept all afternoon."

"I know. "

" We didn't even eat today."

" I know, I'm hungry."

" Is that all you can say is I know?"

" Damn, I was good."

Vee laugh and slugged him with a pillow. She reached for his pills. Gave him his pills and water.

"Vee."

" Yeah babe."

" I'm starving." Andy poked his belly, like a five year old.

"Chicken or beef."

"Pizza with beer. "

"Chicken and veggies it is."

"Blah. I know what I want for dessert."

"What's that baby? "

Getting his food in the microwave.

"Vee ala mode."

Not sure why, but this made Vee blush from toes to nose. Andy always had a healthy sexual appetite, but today he was like a

Bull. She pretended not to hear him. Gave him his food, in bed.

" Veeeeee."

"Babe?"

" I want dessert first."

"Andy!! Eat your chicken while it's hot."

" Can we, go in the parlor?"

She brought his plate, put it on

Coffee table. When she got back to bedroom, Andy had already gotten himself up and in his chair and was rolling to the parlor.

"Andy!!" She threw her arms around him.

"Take it easy, you've been trying to get in my pants all day."

Vee laughed , she looked at Andy, he was glowing.

"Come on, get some food in that belly."

Andy locked his wheelchair, he wanted to try again. He stood up, it was a maybe a few feet to the couch.

"Andy, be careful."

Andy started to move slowly, each tiny step was agony. Getting to the couch, Andy wanted to sit normal without

falling onto the couch. He turned away from the couch and sat slowly. Vee clapped so hard her hands hurt, she jumped into his lap. Andy smiled at her.

" I knew you wanted me!"

"Oh yeah!"

"Andy, get up."

"Come on Vee, 5 more minutes."

" Andy, your drs appointment started 10 minutes ago."

Andy sat straight up..

" Crap, woman, you need to stay away from me, you are knocking me out."

Vee threw him a look. Andy, laughed.

"Uh-oh somebody is in a mood."

Andy pulled on his jeans, threw a shirt on.

" I'm ready."

Vee looked at him, then shook her head. It works for me, she thought to herself.

She went to grab his chair, when she turned, he was standing and moving forward.

" Babe, that's dangerous, if you are going to that we need to get you a cane or walker. "

" Okay."

Did he just agree to a cane?

" What?"

" We can stop for a cane, on the way home."

Damn, I love when he's agreeable, Vee thought.

" You're not going to argue with me, tell me, you don't need it."

" Nope, I don't want to fall. Let's go."

Vee shook her head.

Andy, made Vee stop six feet from the truck.

" Do you think you can support me, so I don't fall. I just want to walk."

" Of course, Baby, that's a great idea."

They got in the truck, the dr was far, but Andy knew it was time.

I need this, for me.

Vee and Andy got inside.

Andy's doctor was at the front desk, talking with receptionist.

"Andy, it's great to see you, did you just walk from your truck?"

Andy nodded.

" I know the last time you were in here, you were having a hard time adjusting, you started to go backwards. You didn't want to get out of your chair, that it hurt too much. Come on, let's get you in an exam room, you can tell me what's going on."

Andy told the doctor, how yes, he actually had given up, he had no fight in him, he was having a hard time in learning how to eat and walk again.

" I never before worried about foods, I could eat , all of a sudden, I had to log things down, even an apple. I was so frustrated."

The doctor nodded.

" Surprisingly, Andy, you are not alone, that there are so many people, just like you, who are going through the same ordeal."

Vee wanted to help Andy.

"Is there anything, I can do to help him?" Vee asked the doctor.

" There are truckloads of books, that give instructions from therapies, cooking to self-care.

The one, who has to do it, is Andy. Help him, guide him but he has to do it on his own. Even little pushes may seem to him, you are trying to change him, he will resent it. Just be there for him. I'll email you a list of books that might help."

Vee made a new appointment and they were on their way.

" You take good care of me Vee, I love you so much."

Vee reached across the seats, caressed the back of Andy's neck.

" We'll get there babe, together."

"Vee?"

"Hmmm?"

"Do you think we could have Tyler over sometime, for like Sunday dinner?"

" Sunday dinner, you mean when my sisters come over, sure."

" Yeah, you know, maybe he'd like the company."

"Okay."

Andy went to call Tyler, he really liked the guy, he seemed real.

Tyler answered the new number coming through his phone remembering, it was Andy's.

" Oh no, you're not a stalker, right?"

Andy laughed.

" No, but I use to be a reporter, so maybe I'm trying to get the scoop on your social life."

It was Tyler's turn to laugh.

" Social life, huh? How about

Wheel dancing, it's new down the Civic center? Are you asking me out, Levesque?"

" What? Nah, man. You're too ugly for me. How about coming over Sunday? We usually have Sunday dinner around 2:30.

It's just me, Vee and her sisters and one their husbands ."

" Yeah, sure why not. Should I bring anything?"

" No, Just your appetite."

" Okay, see you Sunday."

Andy hung up, I like him, he thought to himself.

Chapter 9

Tyler couldn't help himself, he was nervous, he wasn't foolish. Andy was trying to fix him up, like it hasn't happened before, all his wrestling buddies tried, not that haven't been a few sparks but nobody stuck.

Now Tyler, was starting to panic, he wondered if the girl knew she was being set up. Oh well, I'm just going to get a home cooked meal with my new friends, Andy and Vee.

Looking in the mirror, once last time saw, the strong facial features and lean body. He knew he looked good. Grabbing his key, checking to be sure everything was off, here goes.

Anna looked at her watch, she knew that Vee was trying to set her up. She just hated blind dates, though it wasn't a date, right? It was just Sunday dinner.

I could bail early if I get uncomfortable, Anna thought to herself. Who knows he might be, Mr Right, right? Stop talking to yourself Anna.

Anna finished her makeup and started on her hair. Vee loved these Sunday dinner/ get togethers, "my sister, the social butterfly." Anna said out loud.

Me, on the other hand, when you've had your heart shattered, the walls go up. Anna tried not to think about Mickey. She sighed to herself, a waste of four years of my life. "This is why, I don't trust men anymore" again out loud to nobody. I really need a pet, a cat or a dog? You are stalling Anna, yes that's what I'm doing. I think I'm doing a pretty good job at it too. Anna laughed, she did the finishing touches on her make up.

" There! Magnificent."

Anna sighed.

" Yeah, tomorrow, I'm going to the shelter."

Grabbing her keys, another Quick look in the hallway mirror.

"Anna Shaw, you got it going on girl. " she paused " Definitely the shelter tomorrow."

Out the door, walking up to her car, flat tire. Is the world against me, she thought calling Triple A.

Sitting in the car, calling her sister, she could her the conversation now.

" Anna, where are you?"

" I've got a flat, Vee. I'm waiting for Triple A."

" Great, that could be hours."

"The guy just called he's around the corner. It'll only take 5 minutes, come on Vee, give me a break, did I know I was going to have a flat?"

"Well, if you left earlier, instead of 5 minutes before we eat."

Anna sighed.

The Triple A guy showed up.

" Vee, I'll be there in 15 minutes."

A car pulled in front of tow truck.

A handsome guy got out.

" Need some help?"

Anna thumbed the tow guy.

" Oh that was for you, gosh do I feel like an idiot."

"Atleast, you stopped that makes you a good person."
" Yeah, you're right ."
" Always."
The guy laughed.
...

Chapter 10

Maddie had gone outside to check on Tiny, Moose greeted her.

"Hey Moose how is the patient?"

Moose went back to cuddling Tiny.

Maddie sat down on the ground next to Tiny's head. Tiny was doing a whole lot better, he tried to stand, but was a little weak.

I'll take it, he's still here, Maddie thought to herself.

I could just sit here forever, me and my dogs.

Maddie thought about Jesse, how when she was attacked, he moved himself in. He's a good man, I can't wait to be his wife, we may live like husband and wife already but I want to be married before the babies come.

Babies, what's going on in my brains, today.

" Is this seat taken?"

Maddie looked up, Paul, my future father-in-law. It wasn't hard to know what Jesse would look like in the future, he was the spitting image of his father.

" Only by you, handsome."

Paul sat down, next to Maddie,

he turned to look at her.

" How you holding up, kid?"

" I'm okay, just trying to wrap the whole thing around my head. Will I worry about Jess, everyday for the rest of my life now, he's a marked target."

"Yeah, but he always was. "

Maddie looked at Paul.

"Maddie. Jesse, well he's Jesse and he's a mean SOB, when it comes to the law, here in Poland.

He's made some enemies, a lot of enemies, some you know, some you don't, some you really don't want to. That's who he is, Sheriff Jesse Wiseman."

Maddie laughed softly.

" Paul, are you trying to make me feel better?"

" I'm trying to get you to understand, these punks have been around long before you came and will be here long after Jesse's retired. It's the job, just like Benny, Benny use to tell us his job was his calling, I'm beginning to think he was right.

I'm a cop, I'll think like a cop til the day, I die. It's a hazard of the job. Don't worry about Jess, because if he has to worry about you, worrying about him, it's going to distract him and with Lynne out, I don't think he can afford that distraction."

" His father knocked up his partner, you know? Who does these things."

Inside, Dorie was just finished cleaning up the kitchen and leaned against the counter. Max came into the doorway, which he just about filled, with his muscular 6'3" 260 pound frame.

" Hi Baby"

Dorie looked at the man, she had fallen in love with.

" Well, hello there, tall , dark and handsome. Don't you look like the cat that swallowed the canary."

Max gave her a quick look, like what?

" Me?"

" Alright, Max, spill it. You are worse than the kids trying to hide something."

"Baby, I'm stunned"

Just then squeals of joy, echoed through the house.

"KITTENS"

Dorie heard her kids yell. Her eyes flew up to Max. Suddenly, Max was afraid of his tiny mate.

"Ummmm, I didn't know they were home..I screwed up. I wanted to ask you first. I swear."

"Ughhhh" Dorie went to go pass Max, and gave him a small punch in the gut, which probably hurt her hand more than his rock hard abs. Alls Max could say was "Babe". But Dorie looked at him, and sighed.

" It's okay, it's already done."

" I found them on the side of the ride in a box."

"Damn."

" I really was trying to ask you first."

"I know, come on let me see the extra work, you brought me home."

One look at Dorie fell in love, 3 teeny tiny kittens. Each of her kids holding one. Claiming them.

That is until, she saw, the reason why, the people tried to get rid of them.

" Maine Coons."

" Yeah, we have one in Minnesota, the size of a small dog."

" Yeah, but they are gentle."

Just then little Noah, come up to them. Thrusting the tiny kitten, at them."

" This is Charlie, he's my friend."

Dorie just looked at Max and nodded.

" Wow, Mama loves your new friend!" Dorie said to Noah, which made Katie and Scott come over with their kittens.

All three kittens had beautiful markings for Coons. Then, Dorie got serious.

" Okay, they can stay, here's the deal, you three need to help feed and clean up after them okay."

All three kids nodded, like little soldiers. Dorie turned to Max.

" You too."

Max nodded too, like a little kid.

"Grandpa's home!!!!"

The kids ran out with their kittens. The next thing you hear is a big adult squeal. " Kittens!"

Paul Wiseman was a bigger kid than her kids. Dorie fell against Max, trying to hide her laughter.

"Still mad at me?"

" Max, I wasn't mad at you, kittens are a lot of work."

" I know, and I'm sorry I wasn't quick to ask you first."

" Do you think, I was going to say no?"

Actually, Max knew Dorie was going to say yes, or he would have took the kittens to the stables.

" I plead the fifth."

" Oh yeah, well this lawyer is going to make you pay for that tonight."

" Oh no, I'm terrified."

"Goof."

The next thing you see is Paul running through the house, three kittens, his arms.

" My kittens." With the kids running after him.

Dorie looked up at Max.

" See, you unleashed his inner child."

Max laughed and scooped Dorie in his arms. Paul ran through the kitchen again. " KITTENS." The kids on his heels. The four of the running up the Lynne, who looked at Paul and shook her head, he held up the kittens.

"KITTENS!"

" Give the kids back their kittens, wait, when did we get kittens.

Max, Dorie and Paul laughed at her. Noah walked up to Lynne.

" Grandma, Grandpa is crazy."

Lynne laughed, picked up the little boy.

" What did you call me?"

" Grandma."

Noah looked at Katie and Scott for help. The other two kids nodded.

Now, all the adults were misty eyed. Lynne kissed Noah, went over and fake yelled at Paul,who looked sheepishly at his future wife.

The kids ran outside, and the adults all broke out laughing.

Chapter 11

Anna looked in the mirror.

"Jeezz Anna, what is wrong with you? You would think you were going to the prom, it's just a date, with a nice guy. " A nice sexy guy with soulful eyes, that she hasn't stopped thinking about since Sunday.

It was Saturday, Tyler and Anna agreed to get some dinner and catch a movie. She could have kissed him again, when he said.

she could choose the movie. All the guys, she ever dated one thing, to get in her pants, unless Tyler planned otherwise after the movie, he was sweet.

Of course, she could picture, them not seeing the movie because they were too busy making out. Making out? Are we 15 again, Anna banana?

Fifteen, she was captain of her Varsity cheerleading squad, honor roll student, student president of her class, little ms popularity ,dating the captain of Varsity football team, jerk. Anna would

NOT to go back to the good old days, she hated who she was back then, she hated the person she became hurting others just to please her friends. Suzette and Vee were not like that, though both popular and honor students, they were kind and treated people with respect. Anna fell into the wrong crowd trying out for cheerleading and that was freshman year. By sophomore year, she was named co-captain, then it happened the boys started noticing her more and more, over that summer, one boy tried to force himself on her, luckily someone had spotted them and yelled, the boy took off. The guy who yelled, happened to be a drummer in the high school band, Anna brushed herself off, he asked if she wanted him to walk her home, she was shaking like a leaf. " No, I'm fine, thank you." Running all the way home, never telling a soul. That week, she asked her parents if she could quit cheer and take up karate, she was now a master with her own Dojo.

Anna looked back in the mirror.

" That's right, Anna, you can never go home again."

Tyler, looked in the mirror.

" Dude, what's wrong with you, she's just a girl , and you're going to a movie. " The most beautiful girl, Tyler ever laid eyes on, he can't stop thinking about her. I haven't been this nervous since my first make out date, my brothers would have a field day, to know, I feel like puking my brains out, right now.

They did all those years ago, Tyler doesn't even remember the girl's name, but I remember.

I was 17, everyone called me a late bloomer. The girl, no name, was experienced, one of his friends fixed him up, saying it was a "sure thing". He was so green, he actually said " sure thing, for what." Tyler got a huge laugh, for that and no answer.

He borrowed his dad's car and picked up the girl, she had suggested they go to their local "lover's lane", Tyler kissed girls before but this girl was older, he felt pressured, she wasted no time making out and suddenly reached for his buckle. Tyler jumped up and got out of the car." What are you doing?" The girl licked her lips. " Come on handsome, it's already paid for."

Tyler heard laughter, turned to see his so called friends , filming them. " Get out."

The next day, Tyler joined a gym, he was already on his wrestling team, but he was overweight. He loved to wrestle and coach told him to get his weight down, that he had a shot at All State, his parents approved.

No longer, having friends, Tyler concentrated on his workouts and his wrestling, the guys who made fun of him, were the same ones who had to wrestle him.

Tyler won every match, he was on to All State in his senior year.

However, his eye had been on a bigger picture . The WWE.

Joining a wrestling school, scouts talked to him, he knew it was only a matter of time, then it happened, that faithful day, he went to hang out with some buddies.

Tyler's brother and roommate Buddy stuck his head in the bathroom.

" Tyler, stop daydreaming, don't be late for a first date."

Tyler shook his head.

" Thanks man."

" You overthink everything, brother, you look good."

" I was back in high school."

" Awww Tyler forget that, you are not that kid anymore."

" I know, I gained about a hundred pounds since then. "

"Yeah, of muscle. Go have fun, huh?"

" Who are you and what did you do with my brother Buddy?"

The brothers hugged. Buddy patted Tyler's butt.

" Go get her, Ty."

" Thanks man."

Tyler took a deep breath and went out the door. Here we go.

Chapter 12

Saturday, Andy thought to himself, one more day at the gym and he gets a day off. Sunday, was usually the dinner with Vee's sisters, Suzette had a shower to go to and Anna said her and Tyler may go somewhere, if their date goes well, today. Maybe, I should sleep all day tomorrow, before that little red head kills me. Laughing to himself, he didn't see Vee come up behind, she smacked his ass. " Move it, Levesque." she ran out the door, ahead of him. " Come and get me, big boy. Andy laughed harder.

" You know the doctor said I should get my full range of motion back, right."

"Yeaaahhhh."

" Then you're gonna start training, right?"

" For what?"

" Cause, you're going to have run a whole lot faster than that to get away from me."

That shut Vee up.

Andy laughed again, he got to the car, Vee was driving, she turned the car around.

" Where are you going, baby, the gym, is the other way."

" We are playing hooky today."

"What? What did you do to my girlfriend? Oh, I see, you don't want me to get stronger now, so I can't catch you."

She laughed.

" You never know. "

Andy sat in the passenger seat, all he could feel was love for the woman, sitting next to him, his heart swelled.

" We are going to Massachusetts?"

"Maybe."

"Vee, we just crossed over the boarder of Mass."

"Oh, did we? I didn't notice. Oh no."

"Did you check the gas? We have to go back."

Andy groaned.

" You know we checked the gas, you are trying to change the subject."

" What subject is that?"

" Where.. Vee!"

Vee laugh.

" Just sit there, take in the scenery, calm your butt, Levesque."

"Levesque?"

Vee laughed at him.

" Okay, just relax, I'm not taking you to a doctor. "

Andy can't say that was a relief, this little fireball could be sneaky, at times, out of love, but still. He let out a huge sigh.

" Fine."

" Andy, it's okay. You will like where we are going."

Andy closed his eyes.

" Vee, I just wanted to to get better, that's why I'm so jumpy."

Vee reached over, and scratched the nape of his neck.

" You will, baby, we will beat this together."

It's been a long time since Andy was in Massachusetts, he took in the changes on Route 1, guess times really does await no man.

So many memories.

Andy reached for Vee hand and brought to his lips.

" I love you, baby."

"Aww Andy, I love you too, see how relaxed you are. You needed to do this. Stress is a big factor in this disease. I was happy you quit the paper, but now you need to tune into you. Okay."

" I know baby."

Vee got yo Charlestown. Andy's radar went up. It was

October 4th and it was around the time for the Bruins to open their season. Vee turned right on the bridge, onto Causeway street. Andy looked at her.

" Really?"

Vee nodded.

"Yesssss."

" Baby, pull over. "

"Why?"

"Garden pretzel?"

"Andy!"

"One, we can split it. Please."

" Okay. Fine. "

Andy was like a kid in candy store. Vee got out quickly.

" Here."

Andy went to break it, Vee waved him out.

" You can have it. "

" You sure. Are you trying to kill me?"

Vee laughed.

" Your sugar numbers have been amazing. It's okay. The doctor said you can, I can loosen the reigns. "

Andy looked at Vee, he loved her so much. I could be mad, he said to himself, she didn't tell me earlier. I know she is trying to do what's right. Andy grabbed his cane.

" Here we go Bruins, Here we go."

Vee and Andy went in, thank goodness for the escalator. Going to their seats, Andy took in the new arena, he missed the old Garden, but this was nice.

"Vee, do you smell that?"

She just looked at him, she smelled a lot of things.

" What's that babe?"

" Ice baby Ice."

Vee laughed so hard, she almost peed.

They had a great time, Bruins won in overtime 5-4.

Chapter 13

Get it together, Juneau. Tyler thought to himself, it's just a date, you've had hundreds of them. He looked in his rearview mirror. Said out loud to no one.

" Not with Anna, not with the most beautiful woman, I ever saw."

Tyler laughed at himself. Actually, he met Vee before Anna, he had been jealous of Andy, then there were 3 of them.

Get it together Juneau, it's going to be okay. Tyler pulled up, in front of Vee's place, grabbed the flowers on the front seat. When he got to the front door, the panick hit Tyler all over again, he grabbed the railing on the small porch. Anna opened the door, just in time to grab Tyler's arm, she helped him inside.

" Tyler?"

" Panic Attack."

" Oh no, I won't say it's just, I know that's doesn't help"

Tyler smiled weakly.

" I'm sorry Anna."

" Sorry for what? Don't even say that. A lot of my clients start out with anxiety, I know what panic attacks can do."

" Well, I guess you don't want to go.."

" Really? You think I'm that shallow? Just because, my looks, that I'm some kind of snob? First, you thought I wouldn't go out with you because you are an amputee, now you think, I'm so stuck up, I'd dump you, over a panic attack. Give me a break."

Well, if this date wasn't over before that, it's over now. Tyler went to get up, he tried to think of something to say, something other than sorry. He looked at Anna and shook his head, then dropped his head down.

" Tyler." Anna grab Tyler's arm, pulling him into her, kissing him.

" Anna."

" Don't do that again, I am crazy about you, Tyler Juneau. I know we just met but I can't see life without you."

" Me too Anna me too. I think I'm in love you."

" Good cause I know I'm in love with you."

They stayed in, ordering Chinese and stayed up all night talking.

Chapter 14

Jesse had been working, all kinds of crazy hours, he felt bad leaving Maddie on her own so much, she wasn't alone, but he knew she missed him. Doug told Jesse, he needed the night off to go home and be with your family, shut your damn phone off, we will be fine . Jesse agree to the night off, he was exhausted, of course shutting his phone off was something he couldn't do, but he knew Doug wouldn't call him.

" Alright man. I'm outta here."

A cheer went up in the background, all his team mocking their boss.

" Don't miss me too much."

" Take as much time as you need Jess."

" Yeah, I might just do that."

Jesse walked slowly to his squad car. He'd have someone come by and pick in up, he knew he'd be out for awhile, not only did he worry about his exhaustion, he worried about Benny. Jesse worried about Maddie, worrying about him, she probably wasn't wrong. There was so much going on in his life, some days his head hurt. Doug is more than capable, Jesse knew this, it was Lynne that took control, when Maddie got attacked, but it was Doug that was there for second shift, he practically slept at the station.

Pulling into his driveway, Jesse parked, suddenly a sight for sore eyes, Tiny came around the house with Moose yapping at him. Getting down on the ground, he wrestled with the two pups. Paul came out.

" What the hell is going on out here, Lynne is going to skin the three of you alive? Jesse? Shouldn't you be working?"

" Taking a little time, dad. "

Andy got up and brushed himself off.

" Where's Mads?"

" Her and Dorie took your brother food shopping, if you ask me they are training him."

" Oh yeah, sounds right."

Maddie pulled up either way the whole gang. The kids flew out of the car.

" Uncle Jesse" they screamed.

Jesse loved when the kids called him Uncle Jesse like on the Dukes of Hazzard. Truth is, from work, Jesse hardly saw his nephews and niece, it was hard on him. Noah tried to climb up Jesse's body, he pretended to go down from Noah's strength.

" Monkey pile on Jesse" Paul yelled. The kids went nuts, even the dogs jumped on Jesse, looking up Jesse saw his brother standing over him, laughing, in the next minute Benny cleared the kids and jumped on Jesse. The two men rolled around a bit, laughing, getting up Jesse feigned exhaustion. Maddie went over to him.

" Okay guys, the Sheriff needs some air."

The kids ran in the house, to make sure their kittens were okay. Charlie and no names.

The adults followed, Jesse grabbed Maddie pulling her close, kissing her deeply. When Maddie came up for air .

" Wow." Jesse laughed.

" Oh and it's not Sheriff, just Jesse, for awhile."

Maddie looked at Jesse, trying to understand, what he just said.

" What?"

" I'm on leave."

" Leave?" Like Jesse was speaking a foreign language.

Jesse picked Maddie up, throwing her over his shoulder, fireman style. Maddie squealed.

" Leave, as get use to me being

home for awhile. I'm yours."

" Mine?"

Jesse put Maddie down in the doorway.

" Mads!!"

" You mean it?"

"Yeah, I'm taking some time off."

"What happened? "

" I don't know, one minute Doug was telling me to go home for the day, the next minute, I told him to come pick up my squad car. I just wanted to to be there

for you, for Benny, for the kids.. you know they are growing up so fast. I miss them. I miss my family."

" We miss you too, baby."

Jesse hugged Maddie, so tight.

" Jesse, you are breaking me.

Come on, let's get some food in your belly, gotta fatten you up."

" Mama, you can do whatever you please, I'm yours."

" Yes, you are don't you forget it."

Chapter 15

With Jesse home, the next two weeks flew by, decorating for Halloween. The Wiseman home was always decorated for holidays but Halloween, they wanted the kids to have a good time, they threw a little Halloween party. Old school style. Haunted house, bobbing for apples, popcorn balls and candy apples, drawing contest and costume contest plus a bunch of carnival type games for kids. Of course, the head organizers, Jesse and Benny, Dorie and Maddie couldn't be happier, the two men even had a war room set up, for planning.

" This is like the Christmas Bizarre but outside." Dorie said.

" Yep, we have a week and half to go, I can't image what else those two can think of." Lynne said.

" Oh give them time." Maddie laughed.

Tyler knew that this had to be a dream, he would have called Buddy to pinch him to make sure he wasn't dreaming. That would hurt. Tyler just got off the phone, the caller was from an elite wrestling school here in Maine. The guy said he was wondering if I was interested in working at the school, as a trainer. Tyler, at first thought it was a joke, just said " Com'on man."

" Excuse me?"

" You are serious?"

" Tyler, I assure you, I am serious, I know with your injury, you thought your wrestling career was over, but I am here offering to atleast keep you in the ring . I believe you have what it takes to make future stars."

" Yes."

" Yes? Great come by tomorrow, I'll get you set up and meet some of the students."

" Thank you."

They hung and that's when Tyler kept saying it had to be a dream.

He called Anna, things had been going so well, since that crazy first date, Tyler knew Anna was the one.

"Tyler?" Tyler shook his head.

" Hey Anna, I just got some great news."

" Baby, I'm in the middle of a class, what's going on."

He apologized and rambled on real quick.

"Tyler! That's wonderful, oh babe, I'm so happy for you. Let's go out tonight after I get home and change. We can head to Skipper's.

" Yeah!"

" Alright, I gotta go, I love you ."

" I love you Anna."

They hung up

Tyler did a little happy dance, even his artificial limbs had an extra kick today.

" Yes!"

Chapter 16

Andy was bored, not a good thing, his mind begins to wonder, of course, it goes to all his weakness . Alls he wants to do is, go back to work.

" Vee, can we go visit Ray today?"

" Sure, baby, just let me finish some stuff and change. Do you want me to drop you off and I can go visit Suzette."

" Yeah, we can do that."

" Sounds good."

Half an hour later, they were on their way.

" This is a nice idea, Honey, I was going to ask you, if you thought you were ready to go back to work. I mean I can drop you off, you should be able to get around the shop."

" You mean it?"

" Of course, Silly, I'm not the warden, I just wanted to to be okay."

" Thanks baby."

They pulled up in front of the shop, Andy leaned in to kiss Vee.

" I love you, so much."

" I love you too, go to work."

Vee watched Andy, hobble to shop. A month ago, we thought he never walk again, but Andy, he was strong and consistent, even the days, he just wanted to get better and pushed himself through. Vee was super proud of him. She whispered to his back.

" I love you, I will always love you."

Vee put the car in drive and went to see her sister Suzette.

Vee parked outside Suzette's store, it was one of those all in one convenience stores. Vee went inside, Suzette was helping a customer, another customer impatiently waiting at register.

"Can I help you with that."

Vee went around the counter, rung up the sale.

" Have a nice day, sorry about the wait."

The woman thanked Vee and left the store.

Next the woman with Suzette came to the register, looked at Vee.

" Oh, you are twins."

"Triplets"

"My that must of been tough on your parents."

"Sometimes" Vee laughed, but the truth was their parents did struggle at first, but then got a lot of help.

"Well thank you."

"Have a nice day."

Suzette finished helping her customer and came over to Vee, giving her sister, a big bear hug.

" You're hired."

"Are you serious?"

"Yes, I need the help and I don't need to do interviews, I like you.

Vee laughed. " I like to too. It is such a great idea, Andy is down the shoppe, I was just going to hang out. I could use the extra money.

"How's he doing Vee?"

" He's great. You know a tough nut to crack. I taking things day to day."

" Yeah, that's the best you can do. Are you serious about helping out? What time you think you could stay to? I really need a haircut."

Vee laughed.

" I think I can manage. I thought you missed me"

Suzette ran around counter, gave Vee, a huge hug. Grab her purse, and headed for the door.

" Always" blowing a kiss.

Vee called Andy

"Hey."

" Hey yourself, my beautiful

finance', how is Suzette."

" Suzette is fine. She abandoned ship, went to get a haircut."

Andy laughed.

"Frankie was here with Ray, Ray wasn't feeling well, he took him to the doctors. Just me."

" I hope Ray's okay. Andy are you sure you're okay by yourself?"

" Yeah, I feel good. I'm gonna stay til closing. Is that okay? "

" Yeah, that's fine, I'll call Suzette tell her, to get a mani/ pedi too. Call me, if you need anything. I love you."

" I love you too, Vee. I'll talk to you later. Oh, can we swing by the Wiseman's before we go home? I'd like to see everyone."

"As long as you are not to tired, that would be nice."

They hung up.

Tyler was waiting for Anna to pick him up, it was a beautiful fall day, Tyler sat outside on his steps. He watched as Joanne a woman from down the street, was being dragged down the street by a Great Dane.

" What a beautiful dog."

"Thank you, do you want her?"

Tyler laugh.

"Tyler, I'm serious, she's really too much for me, it's you or the shelter."

Tyler looked at her, like really?"

" Shelter? No, she's not going to a shelter."

Joanne handed Tyler the leash, gave the dog, a pat on the head.

" I'll bring her paperwork and crate, by later."

Tyler waved, as Anna pulled up.

"Who is this cutie."

" I don't know her name. I guess whatever we call her."

Anna looked at Tyler and laughed.

" You have puppy?"

" I guess."

" You need a crate."

" No, Joanne is bringing it later. I'm sorry this puts a damper on our plans."

" Are you kidding, Jackie and Skip have a crate in the back room. Let's go eat!"

"Of course, they do."

Tyler kissed Anna.

They got to Skipper's, Anna went in to ask Jackie, if it was okay about bring in the puppy.

Jackie said of course. Anna waved Tyler in. When Jackie saw the puppy, she squealed in delight.

" Oh my gosh, she is beautiful, let me put her in the back, Anna, Clam plate and your friend?"

"Tyler."

" Fisherman platter, I'm starving."

Jackie winked at Anna, as she took little notice no name in the back.

"My kind of guy."

Chapter 17

Andy closed up and waited outside, for Vee. There was a bench they had installed for Ray and himself, when business was slow, they would sit outside eating lunch or talk some.

Andy called Jesse to let him know they were stopping by.

Vee pulled up, Jesse got in, kissed her. Vee looked at him.

" Look at you, I do believe, I see

color, in your face. You look so alive, Andy!

"In one day?"

"Your blood is flowing, I bet you didn't sit down, at all."

Andy looked at her sheepishly.

Vee laughed.

" I was going crazy, Ray had so much new stuff, I had to play with."

" Me too, who knew how busy a little store could get."

Andy took her hand, put it to his lips.

" Maybe, you should stay on with Suzette."

" Yeah, we already come to that. It would work really well, if you want to be coming in here, I could drop you off, until you feel up to driving."

They were soon, at the Wiseman house. Vee just looked awestruck. Andy laughed.

" First time at Wiseman Halloween?"

"Is it BIGGER?"

Andy laughed harder.

"Jesse is home, he is a bigger kid than any kid! Come on, can't wait to see inside."

They got to the door, Andy rang the bell.

"GOOD EVENING" the bell said.

Vee and Andy laughed.

Jesse opened the door.

"Hi guys, come on in. We held supper for you. Hope you are in the mood for beef stew or split pie soup.

Andy stomach growled.

They all laughed again.

Jesse pulled them into a hug. Serious Jesse hugging?

"Come on, let's go feed that stomach, before it barks.

They all went into the dining room.

Tyler and Anna pulled up to Tyler's place, with no name.

" You coming in?"

Anna looked Tyler, Gosh, how did I fall so hard, so fast. They have been together, just about everyday, meeting for lunch or after work. I'm crazy about him, she thought to herself. They haven't been intimate yet, she knew Tyler was concerned she would see his legs.

"Yeah, you got ice cream in this house."

"Three kinds, I'm kinda addicted"

" Me too!"

But, when they got in the door,

the ice cream was forgotten. Tyler was putting the dog in his crate. Anna came up behind him, put her arms around his waist, started to work his belt buckle. Tyler stiffened then relaxed, he turned to Anna.

" Are you sure about this?"

" I've never been more sure in my life. Tyler, I love you."

" I love you too, baby."

Tyler's cel went off, he held up one finger.

"Hello, yeah, what? No, said tomorrow, you need a coach, last minute. Ummm"

Tyler looked Anna. She nodded.

"You don't happen to have a dog crate. Yeah? Great, I'm bringing my girlfriend too. Thanks Bye.

Tyler hung up.

" Anna, I'm so sorry, I shouldn't have picked up."

" Why not? Are you crazy this is your dream?"

Tyler motioned between the two of them.

" So is this" he kissed her, deep and hard.

" Tyler Juneau, you better stop that before I throw you down." He laughed.

"Come on, let's get the puppy, and head to that new gym."

" Tyler, she needs a name."

" You pick, whatever you want."

" Okay, I'll think about it."

Tyler, Anna and no name got to the gym, it was enormous, and beautiful.

" Hey Anna."

Tyler turned to look at the mountain of a man, who called Anna.

"Hi Butch."

"You come to workout?"

"No, I'm actually, with my boyfriend, he's one of the new wrestling coaches. Tyler this is Butch. "

The two men shook hands. Then Butch lit up.

" Tyler Juneau, whoa, Frankie finally found someone, who knows the business. Sorry, about your injury man, Tough break."

" Yeah, thanks."

" Well, see ya guys, good luck Tyler."

Out of earshot. Tyler asked Anna.

" Who was the beefcake."

Anna laughed.

" You're jealous of Butch."

" Am not."

"So jealous, we went to high school together. I do come here, it's my gym."

" You own a studio."

" Yeah, it's not a gym."

" Juneau."

The voice bellowed across the floor.

" That must be Frankie."

He shook the guys hand, Anna took no name and went sit on a bench.

"Anna?"

" Hi Frankie, don't mind me, I'm just here to watch."

For the next, two and a half hours, Tyler was teaching 20 somethings different moves and how they could perfect them. He couldn't get down on the floor, but that didn't seem to matter to his students. Most enthralled that Tyler Juneau was training them.

It was a good day.

Chapter 18

The next 10 days flew by, Maddie was sure that Jesse bought up all the candy in the state of Maine. She loved having Jesse, she knew it wasn't a forever thing. I'll take what I can get, Maddie thought to herself, she looked out, to see Tiny and Moose running around. Thank God. It was nice of Andy and Vee to stop by for supper. Jesse had to show them every new thing he and the kids put up. Jesse being around was a huge, huge plus, so many things he can get done tiny women cannot.

Maddie turned away from the window, in the next second, she nearly jumped out of her skin.

Gunshots. Paul was outside, in a heart beat.

" Maddie call 911 and Doug fast."

Maddie was frozen

"NOW." Maddie jumped and called. Paul wasn't in the mood to shoot anyone.

"Don't move" the guy kept running, the guy fired a wild shot back, Paul went to lift his gun.

There was a blast behind him, the guy went down.

" DADDY! " Paul heard the ambulance.

It was Dorie, Paul and everyone ran in the direction of Dorie's scream. They all turned the corner to see Benny performing

CPR on Jesse. Paul caught Maddie as she fainted. The medics ran over to the scene, Doug and about 6 other deputies showed up. Doug told the deputies to tape off the seen.

"Maddie" Jesse spoke weakly.

Maddie had just come around.

Benny called her.

" He's calling you."

Maddie ran over

" Jesse, Jess, I'm here."

"Mads, I'm okay, it hit my shoulder."

"Ok, Jesse, no more talking, they are taking you to the hospital, I'll be right be.."

" You can ride with us, Maddie."

It was Lisa, Paul's friend's girlfriend.

" Lisa, thank you."

"Thank Benny, Jesse was hit in the shoulder, but the bullet nick an artery, Benny put his knee on the wound to stop the bleeding and started CPR, when Jesse heart slowed from blood loss.

That was amazing."

 Maddie turned around and hugged Benny so hard, got into the ambulance.

Doug, saw the ambulance off,

came back up to the front of the house. Looking at Paul, he asked to see his gun.

"I didn't shoot him, Doug."

Paul handed over his gun.

"So if you didn't shoot him, who did?"

Lynne came up behind Paul.

She passed Doug her Shotgun.

" I did, he was shooting wildly, he could have hit more of my family. He shot my son and aimed at Paul, I'd do it again if I had to."

Lynne gave Doug the shotgun and her badge.

" I didn't ask for your badge, Lynne"

Lynne and Doug were close, they grew up together, went to college together, followed their dreams together, not romantically, as best friends.

Lynne knew taking her badge, is killing him.

" You're the sheriff now Doug. Even if Jesse comes home, when Jesse comes home, I don't know if he'll be back."

" What? That's crazy. Come on Jesse…."

Lynne looked at Doug, but he went on.

" They are not going to fire you, Lynne, it was a justified shot."

Lynne put her hand on her stomach.

" I'm not coming back Doug, send me my papers."

" Shit."

" You'll be fine"

Lynne took Paul's hand, and went into the house.

www.ingramcontent.com/pod-product-compliance
Lightning Source LLC
Chambersburg PA
CBHW040912010826
48978CB00013BB/1263